Puss in Boots

Adapted by Rob Lloyd Jones
Illustrated by Gemma Román

Long ago, three brothers lived on their father's farm.

All day, they dug and planted and carried in crops.

"My sons," croaked
their father, one afternoon,
"it's time you had a reward."

He gave his eldest son the snug farmhouse.

Creak, creak

He gave his middle son the creaky old mule cart.

All that was left for Tom was
the faithful farm cat, Puss.

"Oh Puss, how will I make my fortune now?"

But Puss was a very **clever** cat,
and she had a **crafty** plan.

"First, get me
some clothes."

Puss looked dashing in her stylish black hat...

...her swishy red cape...

...and high, leather boots with shiny buckles.

"Now for my crafty plan," she purred.

First, Puss set a trap for some rabbits. Her whiskers tingled as she waited... and waited...

...and then she
POUNCED.

Next, Puss set a trap for some birds.
Her ears twitched as she waited... and waited...

...and then she POUNCED.

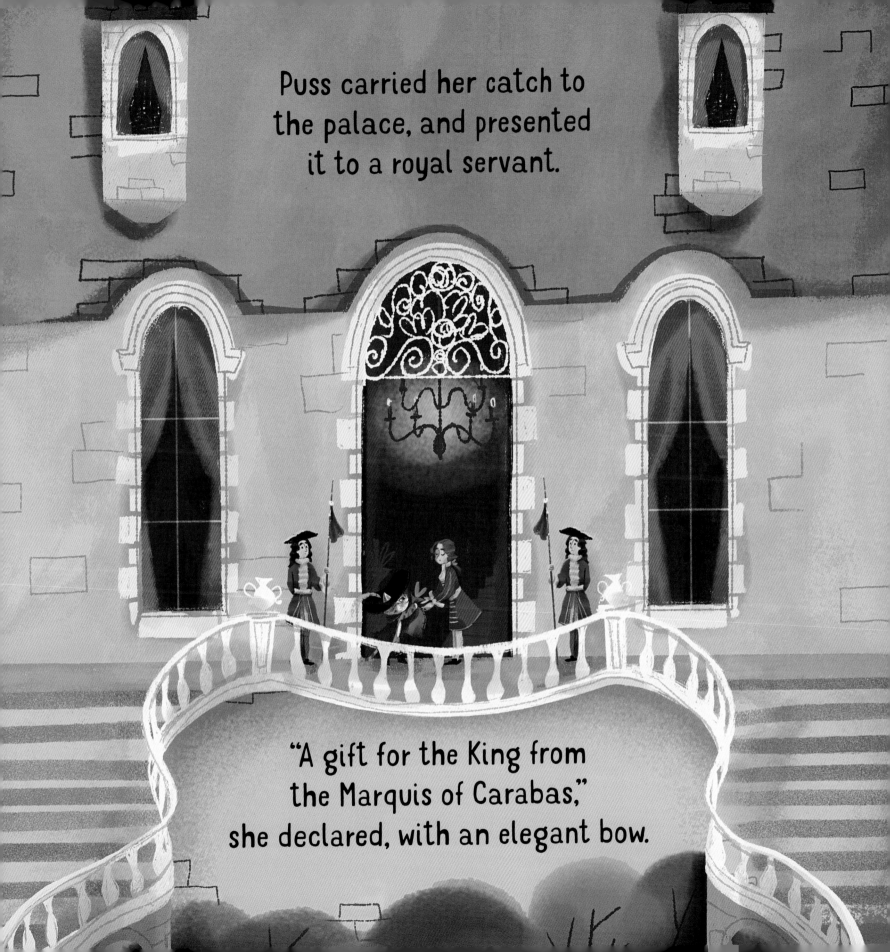

Puss carried her catch to
the palace, and presented
it to a royal servant.

"A gift for the King from
the Marquis of Carabas,"
she declared, with an elegant bow.

Over supper that evening, Puss shared her plan.
"But who IS the Marquis of Carabas?" asked Tom.

Puss's eyes gleamed in the flickering light.
"Soon, it will be YOU," she replied with a grin.

The next day, Puss took Tom to a river.
"Quick! Go for a swim," she said, just as a carriage
rattled past carrying the King and Princess Alice.

"Stop, please stop!" Puss called to the driver.
"The Marquis of Carabas has been robbed!
Someone has stolen his clothes!"

"The Marquis of Carabas?" said the King.
"You gave me a kind gift. Allow me to help you."
And he sent to the palace for spare clothes.

"Now, follow me," said Puss, "for a
feast at our fabulous castle."

CLACKETY-CLACK
went the carriage, as it trundled
between golden fields.

Puss knew this land belonged
to a wicked old ogre...

"When the King drives by, tell him this land belongs to the Marquis of Carabas."

Puss ran to a huge stone castle.

BANG! BANG! BANG!

went her paw on the great
wooden door...

The doors burst open and out stomped the ogre!
His head was as big as a boulder, and his
angry eyes glared at Puss.

"I thought you were meant to be scary," said Puss.

"Watch this!" the ogre boomed.

With a grunt and a growl, he turned into a...

snarling lion.

"Impressive," said Puss, "but I bet you can't turn into a MOUSE."

With a scurry and a squeak, the ogre turned into a tiny brown mouse.

Puss licked her lips...

...and then **POUNCED** and gobbled him up.

Puss bowed to the King with a flourish of her hat.
"Welcome to our castle," she said.

"What a magnificent home!" Princess Alice exclaimed.
"And the Marquis owns so much land!" said the King.

Under twinkling candlelight, they feasted on fried fish, roast meat and slabs of salty cheese.

Tom and Alice talked and talked...

...and laughed and smiled and told
each other lots of funny stories.

"I think they like each other,"
whispered the King.

A year or so later, they decided to get married – all thanks to that crafty, clever Puss in Boots.

Designed by Samantha Barrett
Edited by Jenny Tyler and Lesley Sims

Digital manipulation by John Russell